HOW HIGH?
—THAT HIGH

HOW HIGH?
—THAT HIGH

stories

DIANE
WILLIAMS

SOHO

The following stories have appeared in *Harper's Magazine*: "What Is Given with Pleasure and Received with Admiration?" "She'll Love Me for It," "How High?–That High," "Inserted into the Rest of Her," "Master of the Blast," and "Feel and Hold."

The following stories have appeared in *Granta*: "Più Vivo," "Tale of Human Adventure," "Grief in Moderation," "One Muggy Spring," "Secretly Try," and "Thanks, Dot."

The following stories have appeared in *London Review of Books*: "How Much Did You Ever Think the World of Me?" "Molly Went Along Quickly," "Have a Seat in the Big Black Chair," "With This New Greasiness," "I'm Sure I Love and I Really," "Harriet Mounce," and "Stick."

These stories first appeared, sometimes in a slightly different form, in *BOMB*: "Outcome," "The Prayer of the Primogenitor," and "A Worthy Companion"; in *Conjunctions*: "Popping" and "Flowers, Birds, and Gardens"; in *Image*: "Upper Loop," "Sight See," and "It's So Effortful"; in *Lake Effect*: "Nick Should Be Fun to Be With"; in *Mal*: "A Type of Vertigo"; in *MIRonline*: "Captured!"; in *New York Tyrant*: "Finished Being"; in *The Paris Review*: "O Fortuna, Velut Luna" and "Garden Magic."

Published by Soho Press, Inc.
227 W 17th Street, New York, NY 10011

Library of Congress Cataloging-in-Publication Data
Names: Williams, Diane, author.
Title: How high? - that high : stories / Diane Williams.
Description: New York : Soho Press, [2021] Identifiers: LCCN 2021011524

ISBN 978-1-64129-306-8
eISBN 978-1-64129-307-5

Subjects: LCGFT: Short stories.
Classification: LCC PS3573.I44846 H69 2021 | DDC 813/.54—dc23
LC record available at https://lccn.loc.gov/2021011524

Printed in the United States of America

10 9 8 7 6 5 4 3 2 1

To
Christine Schutt
Wolfgang Neumann

I like to take charge and usually things turn out right.

—ANONYMOUS

CONTENTS

UPPER LOOP

———◆———

I am trying to think if there's any reason for having fun anymore on any level? I know that that's not the kind of thing people usually talk about. God forbid—so I scale the roof all the way to the ridge and I have never had to climb down.

GARDEN MAGIC

———◆———

I took a step further to meet Horace for health, for love, for a leg up.

And at Horace's everything was gray there with some white accents—and the walls were gray, not paint. They were hung with fabric and he had a gray carpet on the floor.

Once, before I knew him well, I asked Horace to dinner and after that he was always saying that he'd be right over for a chicken dinner, but usually I visited him in his apartment across the street.

His place was very tidy and a bit surprising. He showed me his sword cane and his living room features an owl that's made of poultry feathers.

This is a snowy owl that contains no real owl parts, but when I saw it for the first time—I had to ask whether it had been shot or euthanized.

We got married and I should explain that I am tiny—a kind of skinny woman.

You see, Horace says he likes to think of me as a young sailor boy or he may refer to me as a china doll and, for short, call me China.

I moved in with him, and not long after, we waited in line to see the Czech film *Valerie and Her Week of Wonders*.

And when we both saw Lila Melinek in the line up ahead, Horace stuck a finger between the cheeks of my backside.

Even with my coat on, I was very much aware of the point of pressure.

One day Lila forced her way into our apartment while I sat alone in another room. It was a bold and moody time.

I heard Lila tell Horace, "The trouble with you!"

"I'll try to be a better friend," Horace told her, "but I need to be with someone who knows French."

I am that one. Oh, otherwise I heard murmurs and I did walk in to join them where they sat.

Lila's hair hung down her back and I'd like to offer more about her, but I don't know what that would be. She is better than me?

I put myself into a chair and watched them, except some of the time I kept an eye on the owl who also pressed on my nerves.

"When can you go?" I asked her.

"I'll return," she said, and she stood.

And she's not meek, but still she's waifish, with babyish hands and oversize antlike eyes.

I had the impression that Lila wanted to belong to our family and in several ways Lila and I are likely alike, although I'm not one to come up with plausible ideas of myself.

Horace said, after she'd left us, "She's my Georgia peach. What do you want for me?" That's what I thought he said. But what he said was, "What do you want from me?"

Well, she did take him away when she came again.

I am in a room with . . . I am in a room where decisions are unlikely to be thought out, where I lack strong enough character and vital drive to take my dark thoughts and plant them at the right time like spring bulbs.

GRIEF IN MODERATION

———◆———

A necessary and great object of interest—he had first found Valentina standing among other members of her family.

Her clothes were a shocking pink color and as her wet hair dried, it began beguilingly to curl.

And she was fragrant and Tom thought she was showy. She is not common in the wild.

And lots of other people still go up to her and consider her the way Tom does.

Most persistently, she brings into view a face that displays full-bodied welcome.

One weekday evening, in a local restaurant, a very tall drunk man walked over to the pair, kissed Valentina on the mouth, and then departed quickly.

Tom had questions. It was a puzzling capper to a typical day.

Tom, on that day at work, had closed out tax cases upon which no tax was due, and awaited a repairman to discuss the photocopier failure.

And Valentina has responsibility for all of the patients on her hospital shift, as well as the building, and people are responsive to her, sometimes fervently.

She did not respond, however, to Tom's questions. She kept at her meat. She might otherwise have been caught in contradictions, but then she backed up in her chair and she gave her husband her answers: But it isn't true. I don't recall. Sort of. Yes, I sometimes do.

At bedtime Valentina lay on her back, arms at her sides, as did Tom. There was no intertwining and no tender touch that needed to become better still, except that their small-patterned wallpaper seemed to be excited the next morning.

The tiny daisies were scored by the shadows of the slats of the venetian blinds and the stripes were shivering.

And here at dawn was Valentina's instrumental smile! Her sign of sweetness that is the flying start, the fresh impetus, the feature on her face that creates her particular style.

And in theory she well understands any person's right to have privacy; to challenge and to complain without fear of reprisal; to make known his or her wishes; to receive complete information. To be wrenched.

HAVE A SEAT IN THE
BIG BLACK CHAIR

——◆——

I had had enough of everything during what I took to be my turn.

"Can I just pet it," I said, when Tim and I were in bed, "instead of my taking it inside?" But Tim said no.

And then, at the task, he pulled himself back and forth inside of me with many repetitions, enough to get to the next step for him—to stabilize the project. He was cramming rather a lot into the tiny space.

At any rate, in the aftermath, I was catching

a partial view of the white-washed brick wall through the window, and I could see the boxed Dutch blooms that needed deadheading.

The first of the daytime light was hitting the flowers hard—like the big sky lightning that doesn't quit suddenly.

This life with Tim King had come about abruptly and while I am on this subject—what compromises must I continue to make? What are my hopes? Think!

Tim tells me that his memories sting him to death.

I got up, dressed. Had coffee, arrived at work, made telephone calls, and sat at my desk on one leg.

Then they said, "Have a seat in the big black chair," which I did, "and Mr. Damien will be with you shortly."

Mr. Damien has excellent posture and he reminds me very much of Tim who doesn't work here.

I had pangs.

When Mr. Damien arrived, we talked for more than a quarter of an hour about my new stint to check in freight shipments.

The good thing is that my new job is nine to five, since I slow down at five.

The sight of Mr. Damien parting his hair with his hand backfired or exploded as far as

I was concerned because I guess his reaching fingers were twirling—so that I was jittery and I didn't hear every word he said concerning the payroll data.

His hair is blond. His ears are set close to his head. His nose hardly protrudes. His mouth was opening and closing, pouring out the capsule summary of yet another list of my duties.

Well, I will try to take pride in a job well done.

To enjoy the situation will be an effort of a lifetime.

FEEL AND HOLD

———◆———

To get a bit of food, the Rotches went out in the morning. And since the meat at the market didn't look very appetizing—it wasn't cut in the same way we cut meat—they chose not to buy any meat.

The hands of the market vendors were much more expressive than our hands—the hands we have at home. For example, when taking up a piece of merchandise, those vendors' hands could feel and hold at the same time.

When we hold a thing—I am not so sure we feel it.

And at the market, to make the tea that was provided—there was theater involved!

They'd stuff a cup full with mint, put plenty of sugar on top and then decant the boiling water from as much as two feet above the cup!

Rotch was—did I already tell you this?—that my friend Rotch became quite a problem in the end and he fled to some remote part of the country.

What his wife was after was a life of joviality. Joviality—jewelry?

No matter.

They had no carpet on the floor and their floors were all concrete and they always shook out their shoes before putting them on because scorpions might have been in there, inside of their shoes.

In the afternoon at four o'clock, every day in that country, the rains would come and it would rain for an hour, and we could see that the trees had raindrops on them.

Such satisfactions—how in the world did satisfactions ever get into the world?

At the market, Rotch often spoke to a certain man there about a chronic headache or a nightmare. Mrs. Rotch could not keep it to herself either—her affliction—her petulance. *Let's get the food!*

It was hard for them to find each other worthy of respect and Mr. Rotch, I've come to think, wanted a reward for his fidelity, which was not forthcoming.

Mrs. Rotch was often seen straight on—against a wall—with her saddle nose pointed skyward, sitting with her hands clasped on her knees.

I should have called on her more often when she lived alone.

I once tried to pull Mrs. Rotch up onto her feet little by little.

A chair was on its side. A wooden urn had cracked.

I took off her wet clothing. There was a hole in her dress and it was my fault. I was unable to move her. Later I looked in and she was in the same situation.

Now her heart gets so much assistance from a pacemaker that sometimes I think she is unable to die.

Among her own family she should have been safeguarded. I guessed how things would turn out for her.

I made a small effort. If only she had been utterly absorbing.

. . .

There are those who have watched me return from my sojourns, because I am a little homesick, to my native town—that has just about everything—sex, philosophy, politics, and pandemonium.

Here's a custom for you—gawking—and it needn't be heartbreaking.

And even though I am a wispy woman, I believe I have flared up here in Glencoe like a flame—amidst my mother, daughter, husband, and some friends, and that I cause fretfulness.

HOW MUCH DID YOU EVER
THINK THE WORLD OF ME?

He'd never quite seen anyone in that state before, even though he has a mother and all that.

Today Lizzie is, he thinks, irresistibly plaintive.

Then the doorbell jerked the husband to his feet.

Does Lizzie live here?

Who are you?

Where did she go? Where did Lizzie go?

Who wants to know?

Lizzie meant to answer hurriedly and hotly, but nevertheless stayed hidden.

Around here real and imaginary characters are shockingly always crossing paths.

Lizzie clearly identified the lugubrious voice of her first love—a pain in the ass who had become too quarrelsome—who had worked out well in the short run when he could still be funny. Now she should speak to him, say memorable things.

He'll soon be with me, she thought, for his wail had come again at her through the closed door. Then she heard the racket of paper being fought with in an effort to crush it into a ball—or was that the window blind that was shrieking in the next room while being hoisted against its will—or while it was being let down too swiftly?

That sad sack will find me, she thought.

Why did she cling to that notion?—because the tree leaves this autumn in Hubbard Woods, where they live, are falling down as they ought to?—because the dead leaves have the life spirit to collect themselves and to push themselves to go to the necessary places?

Did Chaddy rattle and scatter himself toward me? Did he die? Lizzie asked herself.

A TYPE OF VERTIGO

———

For many years she was in that village in the form of a wife, an unloving wife, and things could not have been improved upon.

How is her husband by the way? Did he actually have a stroke? No, it was just a type of vertigo.

They used to be so close. He knew everything about her.

His brother had two strokes.

The wife is ashamed of herself.

For how long did her bad behavior go

on?—for a time, for some time, perhaps from that time on.

How does this end?—with bits of cake falling from her mouth, into her lap and being brushed by her onto the floor—and then it ends also with her chatter as she further cuts and chips at the man, her husband, whose name is Will.

The weather. It was perfect and the road from her house to the center of the typical town she lives in arcs and descends, lined with hawthorn and poplars, and in spring there are the lilac hedges in bloom.

What else can one see?—a downpour, the rain's beauties, the bits of the wife's butter cake waste on the kitchen floor, not painful to witness, but worms are in peril on pavers after the rain, near the mailbox where some birds or the hot sun might get to kill them. The worms had come up above ground for air.

What else?—no, nothing else—for this brief tour has concluded.

And, it has not been obvious to this twosome to know how or by what means, after which precedent, or to what degree—to be the best sort of spouse.

Yet in another town several miles off, in a high-lying region, other stories of intimacy are, of course, proceeding.

And during a recent sunny day in *that* town—platforms had been erected, framed by booths, for a street fair that a married pair attended where they bought a small ceramic bowl "Made by Marta."

Marta is an expressive human who has a grainy ochre body. She presides over bowls and pitchers and platters that feature striped and convivial decoration. More often than not, Marta gestures and speaks playfully.

Hers is a history that is ancient and fundamental, not like some, like mine, which is—*Please leave me alone so I can just be pretty.*

And will there be anything else, Madame?

INSERTED INTO THE
REST OF HER

———◆———

My arm is scaly and thin and my bracelet has oblong links of fake gold. It's not real. It's not real, and the doctor had his admonitions for us that we kept trying to put into Willy's words or into mine on the walk home.

Oh, what the human body can go and do on its own because there was something really awry with Willy.

We followed a group of children who were also being strongly advised. And there was no varying of the force or the pitch of the voice that was shouting at them—*Don't ever eat the berries!*

I encircled Willy's waist with my arm, but I often brood over whether I am partial enough to my husband who is very ill.

The sun was briefly out and in the gilded city air, we thought to make a stop at The Cherry Door Thrift Shop where we bought a small but heavy chest—handcrafted.

"Do you really want that?" the clerk asked. She took more pride in some practical tables that were light enough to carry.

On foot, with the help of a store hand, we got the chest home in the rain. It was a ticklish scene, decorated by toothy-edged clouds overhead, and the chest has made little atmospheric change in the world of our home.

Doctor Boondas had prescribed glyceryl trinitrate for Willy. And his nurse had waved at us and shut the door behind him when Willy went in. And then another woman cast herself forward through the door toward me.

It looked as if her head and her neck had been carved separately and then inserted into the rest of her. She had a grave aspect and the gaze of a person in a trance.

"I had one!" she shouted at me, as she pointed at and took up my wrist.

She fingered my faux good-luck piece, from

which I count on powerful emanations to pro-
duce certain happy-enough results.

She said, "I gave mine to the church."

And my ornament is common enough. I'd
say one like it can be found in North America
in almost every treasures and trash locale.

I also collect shells.

I found a plaster figurine of a Greek goddess
to stand up in between our books, to keep them
from falling on their faces on the bookshelf.

I did recently give away a full-zip fleece
jacket and a coffeepot percolator. Soon Willy
will go.

I used to think he afforded protection. In
the case of Willy—much like a dragon with a
down-to-earth aura—he was especially feared
and recommended.

My regard for my plaster Artemis is deeply
implanted and she can bring on a blush when I
see her—a hot jealous feeling for her thin neck,
heavy hairstyle, and for the glass spheres inside
of her eye sockets.

PRAYER OF THE PRIMOGENITOR

O nce I was there I wanted out of there, although they served us a plum torte and coffee and it was delicious, with whipped cream and that helped.

We were talking about what was going to happen.

It was really very emotional, while we were eating our sweets and drinking coffee from cups that had been filled from a spiggoted urn.

At the palace of the town hall we still had the electrified Polish chandelier that was fully lit, even though fires, earthquakes, and military attacks have changed this building's appearance.

And a lady was gliding from guest to guest with her hands locked to imply she might be at prayer.

Her mouth was open. The tongue was curling up toward her upper row of teeth and the nose was upturned as well. Her eyes were blue, white, black, and orange and she was ably balancing the lyrical and the dramatic.

She was advancing toward me and I thought, Good God!—when a dog with white, silver-tipped hair threw himself hard at her. She called the dog Electra and gestured it away.

As she reached my side, she said, "Now who is this? Where did you come from?"

I took her hand, surprised myself, bowed slightly and kissed it.

"Bless you," she said.

And so blessed I was—I was wishing that soon I would have the art of making people listen. I'd be talking my way to success. I'd be thinking like a millionaire and know all that I need to know about married life and intimate sex.

I am supposed to hope for things to be right and comfortable in the future, and not long after this, I encountered a big stone when I started my garden.

I did it all by myself getting that stone to loosen up, using a long steel spit about five feet long.

I found a point of leverage, established that big stone in the soil near the road, and put a few smaller stones on top.

And when I pass by my cairn I think about this—that I am a man ready to receive what I deserve—and that I am a man who has this swell erection.

MOLLY WENT ALONG
QUICKLY

—————

E ventually the mother died. My wife was
in spite of everything, very fond of her
mother, and had saved a dog abandoned at
Vaughn's—because, she said, the dog reminded
her of her mother.

Then why be so careless? Because Molly
went up a walkway of stairs with the dog who
wasn't on a leash, and using by-paths—she went
far into a part of the park where there were
high thickets and the dog disappeared.

So after we had given up looking for the

dog and had called the ASPCA—we headed off to get a few things, like some milk and a cucumber.

Vaughn at the Palm Superette told us Tiger had just been there and had eaten a meal of sausage slices, and as it turns out, the dog was on his way home.

He is a smart dog.

He's a cross between a terrier and a whatnot, hardly a hair toward the rear end, a shivering mess and he is constantly peeing on the bedspread and on the table leg.

Oh, it's easy to clean up, Molly says, and it's nothing.

One evening Molly was on her knees by the bed alongside Tiger and I observed her enthusiasm and the refined groping Molly was engaged in with Tiger and she said something jumbly to him.

I found that suddenly I wanted to accuse Molly of anything or maybe I wanted to appeal to her for kindness.

But I took no time at all to choose between these and this is a consequence of the wellsprings of spontaneity that I count on to feel alive.

There were people just like me, I am sure, among the first humans—who rallied themselves to the cause of vibrance and penance.

Tiger stood and moved backward barking

while I said aloud quite loudly what amounted to bad luck for all of us. It brought a blight, a disaster.

And confronted by this and other injuries I've caused—Molly has never left me, nor have I wandered away. I am not ready to bow out. I have no idea yet how this matrimonial entanglement ends. Tiger died. He was such an eager dog.

This morning we were getting ready to travel—I was going through my things to find my wallet and my passport and we were very late—and I found that I had this fantastic feeling!

I am looking for something—my hand is on it—the thing I am looking for! But my hand knew it—*this was not what I was looking for.* And sure enough, it was an old passport.

Then there was an issue with an old greasy toolbox with spare parts, too near the clothing. The toolbox has some importance.

The spare parts that peeked out of the toolbox looked like intestines. I want no part of them, yet I knew we had to keep these.

Besides, I knew we couldn't get going until I found the passport—and the money.

But no matter what, I might have already spent the money rashly, although also probably with a great deal of care.

PIÙ VIVO

———◆———

"Here Mackham!" Molly calls and *"Here I am, poor Molly,"* he replies.

And there is no bitter blaming between them of the kind my wife Molly and I now engage in, such as—*"Don't tell me that I'm wrong! Can't you just say you disagree?"*

Since we live in the city, as does Mackham, it's no trouble to run out and do an errand on foot. And one afternoon, when I left home to steer clear of them—a baby in a stroller rolled by with a crisp attitude that I took to mean she had faith in herself.

One of her legs was up high and she held tightly to a toe.

The posture did not look in the least strenuous and soon she reappeared with both legs up and her feet tucked in beside her ears.

This, of course, was no invitation to me, but I was horrified that I could not think of it otherwise.

Our slider windows were open when I went back home and the air inside smelt of a strong solvent. Mackham was at the piano and I thought he made blunders.

"What is that music?" I asked, and Molly said, *"It's his own!"*

All of its parts to my mind worked in and about one another in confusion and there was little precision in the single parts that composed the whole. And the melody—when it attempted to be the upper voice—failed.

And yet Mackham had the right amount of energy to propel the serenade forward and he asked me what I thought.

"Sounds like the roof work we had done," I said, "but I admire the pace."

Mackham made no reply and kept on with the very discreet and immature demeanor of a child.

A heap of color was in Molly's lap, as she sewed a skirt hem, periodically making the necessary knots. She proceeded with stubbornness of conviction and then with hesitation as she addressed me, *"Sit down! No, go!"*

But it was Mackham who left and I ended up lightly touching Molly and she permitted what I meant to convey.

Pet, *pet*—*pet*—*pet*, *pet*—*pet*, *pet*, *pet*—nothing so unusual—not unlike the sort of casual pampering a dog owner banks on.

But perhaps Molly was appeased as next I launched more delicate and creditable figurations on her body.

Except that she toppled a small, curved and empty flower vase on the table near us as we heard the sound of Mackham. He was returning.

You've seen, I am sure, a performer stock-still on the stage—during which time he waits for his ovation.

This is how I am these days.

Lately and often Molly has spoken to me about Mackham, about how marvelous, about how unheard-of he is, and she allows herself to have such rampant feeling only if I can agree.

A WORTHY COMPANION

———◆———

Did she have a deep cut?—a jagged cut?—minor?—a puncture?—or penetrating. It was penetrating. An unplanned, wavy line of blood pointed the way to the wound.

And she's lovely except that now her eyes look too milky, as if they'd been glued into her head with too much glue. "Would you do me the biggest favor?" she said.

"I think so, no," he said.

Although instantly, he brought her first aid and in a hotel room one night, the case could be made that she is the plaything of the man and that he is hers. They like that idea.

People with all of these goofy ideas still find people and keep them in tow.

This union became a marriage—said to have occurred after a funeral.

Nothing but pyramid-type, green hills all around, day of the wedding, where they stood.

Here's to your!

Here's to your!

The new partners looked around at the steep hills, and next to them, at the extensive plantings, and they heard what they took to be laughing flowers, quieter trees and when the trees are happy they sing plenty of well-known tunes.

In every language there is a story like this— how sometimes people will step out to get a boost from the gist of things.

So therefore, put it into the air!—that the gist of things is "That Lucky Old Sun," "Whispering Grass," and "Oh, Yeah!"

O FORTUNA, VELUT LUNA

———◆———

What is Miss Treece's trouble according to a popular notion?

The man A has failed to show up.

Arousing herself at the restaurant, she fixes her lipstick when her solo supper concludes and takes herself down the stairs situated behind the bar.

There, at her business in the restroom, the foamy hand soap is suggestive of fun, but there's the wringing of her hands and the twitching of her fingers while she washes.

"I never heard. I don't know . . ." another woman was speaking into her phone before clicking it off. And these two women might have briefly inspired one another had they smiled, because they were both disillusioned.

But they might still build temples to themselves of volume and color, as a poet once said.

Happily Miss Treece's home is very well-lit, very inviting, and she keeps the door unlocked so you don't have to hesitate to go in.

Yet it's necessary to walk through her house on a diagonal, because the entryway is positioned at the corner of her parlor.

And, those calls of hers for help were more often ignored because she was also promoting herself behind a lot of jargon and she had recently returned from an extensive tour through Europe where she had lectured people.

But, she is thinking to herself, If A had only said, *Sorry I upset you and I am sorry it's an anxious time for you. I am sorry*—then she would have done what? Taken pride in herself?

She takes a laxative and looks in the mirror at her features, which are stretched stiffly with ingratitude.

Ah yes, and she wonders about visiting

the M'Calmonds on the weekend, but Janet M'Calmond does not like her, not really.

She contemplates her plain-boarded, sloping floor and the autumn fruits on the sideboard and she feels unworthy of them.

She thinks she needs to call A to see how he is, so that he will care about her again. "Is everything all right?" she asks A.

"Of course."

"But you never came to Shangri-la."

"For your sake."

For her sake, forsaken.

She reaches to gather a fold of her nightgown and sees a few light threads that are breaking free at the hem and rudely pulls on one of these. She starts to cry.

This crybaby is a middle-aged woman. And what exactly is a crybaby? She is the picture of a child, angered to have been placed to stand on a chair that is too tall, that she, the tot, all by herself, could not have gotten herself up onto.

And another thing that strikes Miss Treece particularly is her thought about the upcoming loss of all kinds of pleasure.

She begins to cry more, not into the telephone. Her phone call with A had ended because A "had to hop," he'd said.

The accentuated curve of her lower back is causing her trouble—it aches. And if, in the dark, she gets up and out of bed, she'll need to remember where everything is. Remember.

She does remember something that has just happened that has unsexed her.

Well, she turns off the lights and then the lowboy and the carpet and all else can fall into insignificancy.

Around noon one day, she walked and walked while wearing a new pair of shoes that had a bedroom-slipper shape and then she halted at a store window and looked in at table lamps. She thought they were preening, when they hadn't yet distinguished themselves.

The exception was the pair of stone lions, fashioned into lamps that she deemed notable. True enough—except that their overblown frowns announced to her that they were the worst sort of sore losers. Admittedly, she hadn't seen the Three Graces, the minor naked goddesses who were miserably clinging to one another beneath a fringed shade.

A magazine advertisement was holding on to the face of the window for dear life. It made claims that this shop was an excellent source for furnishings, a dependable source, a secret source, a fountainhead, a bedrock, a backbone.

The man B stood behind her saying, "Lena, aren't you Lena?"

"What do you want with me?" she said. And B, a man with no obvious defects, replied, "To tease you."

And Lena Treece said, "You won't mind if we do it right away. It will be a comfort to me."

So during her trek with B through the park to get to his home, Lena Treece saw a seated man with folded hands, a kneeling woman combing her hair, a woman carrying a child, a little girl jumping rope, and a woman with outstretched arms. Certainly these people were lifelike, but God knows (poor Lena doesn't) what their ability is to get along with others, their general intelligence, perseverance, reliability, ethical standards, and which ones have a normal down-to-earth attitude toward all matters and are willing to progress steadily where friendship is concerned.

THANKS, DOT

———◆———

She was so thankful for that cheerful dot in the sky!

And the sighting of the moon served Ms. Coyte well as temporary encouragement. She had been weeping and she does so whenever she can—and it's sad to see how bad this is in what might be viewed as a pleasure house for some.

Gee! The full-size moon gained a victory over the woman—Ms. Dorothy Coyte (née Hiles).

But in the morning, she noted with dumbfoundment the locket that the innkeeper wore, and she thought—*Maybe, if I had bought the one like that one in Philadelphia—everything would have turned out better for me.*

People! People love lockets!

Roderica Dobson, the innkeeper, put her life story forward for Ms. Coyte at breakfast and she was so happy to tell it. Also, Dobson was very beautiful, although the tale she told concerned her severe loss of reputation, as well as an appreciable sum of money.

Even so, the aura of the house produced for both women a touch of comfort and low-key luxury. This was especially the case at the core of the house where the hall walls were covered by wallpaper bearing a pastel lily-pad theme— and there was a broad verandah with chairs.

"Are you married?" Dobson asked while Coyte plied the pastry Dobson called a *kuchen*. *What's a kuchen?*

"Am I married? I don't know," Coyte said. "Have you already eaten?"

"A plum," Dobson said.

And in the crevices and stuck onto her lashes—sand was in lumps all in and around her eyes.

Why didn't she wash the lumps away?—or just pluck them out. *Not the eyes!*

. . .

Dobson was meant to represent, I believe—
with her exceptional physical nature—a nearly
redeeming being. To whom? To me.

Lamentably she's missed her chance. But
just now I have yanked the blue frog out from
a muddle at a street bazaar.

The Blue Frog. When I say those words I
expect a reprieve—a tavern—tranquility.

I see myself in Ireland. We drive and I spot
a road sign—TO THE BLUE FROG and we go in
and have a pint.

You have to look at the glass frog with the
sun on it.

It is the sheer pool of eternity and I would
like the blue frog to go down into my grave
with me.

NICK SHOULD BE FUN
TO BE WITH

———

He has a wife who might reassure him. No doubt she is often sorry for him, so she took his hand.

But for how much longer should she hold it?

She is very knowing about a few things, yet her attempts to embrace her husband ought to have worked out better.

And because she often wishes to be unguarded with Nick in her nakedness, she had taken off her clothing after supper.

And in the aftermath, she had little else to say, except, "I am sorry. You don't say that. Did you hear me?"

She cannot repursue, reuse, or reinspire her husband well, although she is as keen as any to try.

But let the two of them speak more and they discuss such topics as: *the insulting compliment* and *the power of the lie*—for them, easy-to-slide-into-subjects.

In fact their house is also a retreat that is lovely to curl up into. And in the morning, as in a happy story, the wife beats eggs for an omelet, looping up the froth with a fork in a china bowl, and listening with appreciation to the fork tines pit-patting prettily.

And the walls of their home are painted duck egg blue and today a pink geranium in a clay pot is on the dining table.

A library bookcase combines perfectly their pottery, candlesticks—their books of humor, history, biography, and fiction.

As for the wife's periodic lack of sympathy—yes, it's true—she has said terrible things to her husband and to others about him.

And the husband's primary ideas more often than not are about pain and drawbacks—both combined.

So, in order to have intercourse, Nick usually

enters Linda from behind, but not cheerfully enough. And his probes are not pleasurable for either one of them, but their effects linger.

Certainly there is plenty of opportunity to piece together a proper picture of the Demule-meesters. Just a moment ago, they lived, pleasingly ever after, by such a narrow margin.

I'M SURE I LOVE AND
I REALLY

——◆——

I took notice of the protrusion of my wife's mouth that then drooped and of every buttoned-up button on her clothing—and at how she avoided assuming any uninteresting or stiff-looking pose.

With both of her arms overhead, she kept on rising on her toes and then tapping her heels to the floor.

"We're like *this!*" she said, finally stopping her game. She flung her fists together and said, "Now, it's time to go!"

So then we set off to see Nixie Wagstaff who is to my mind never quarrelsome and aggressive the way we are.

Nixie welcomed me, by putting the entire side of her head against my chest.

But tell me what kind of an indifferent animal was that?—too big to be a cat—turning its back on us? It was twisting itself atop a woven willow border fence.

But Nixie is a warm-hearted girl with a glossy, showy face and a chrysanthemum fragrance that's a bit peppery.

She mentioned people's names and nicknames alongside her many comments that began with—*I'm sure, I love* and *I really, really like* and *I know*.

I went alone into the house and into the dining room to get an all-embracing view of the landscape through the long windows. And on the lawn I saw the small sweet forms of the two women, flanked by a pair of hornbeams.

It was another one of those incidental, but unusually pretty scenes that might fulfill for an instant an extreme need I have to be blissful.

Another such scene—a threesome in a glade—with a blossomy border—was pictured on a faded plate that was stowed upright in a dish cupboard.

In another such scene, somebody behind me put an arm across my body at the level of my waist, touched the front of my shirt—and then the darling—and must I need to know which one?—softly laid her hand beneath my belt and let it rest there.

Get a grip. In some other similar scenes two men are fishing or there is a ruined castle gate with cows—a hamlet with a church tower—or a wide stretch of water with a figure walking dogs on the near bank, sheep!—a dock scene with ships, trees in blue, in brown, in purple or in shades of red. Grasses! Clouds! Once a donkey.

Or it's a country house in green appearing to be entirely natural.

WITH THIS NEW GREASINESS

———◆———

One of them breaks the routine at the office usually—mouths off or is sullen, every once in a while.

The man said, "You know why I'm here, Jane."

Jane grabbed at the man where some soft flesh is, with some force, perhaps because so many persons were no longer in her life—not Titus or Roddy, Mamie or Cecelia Bouché— whom she had checked in with and needed to double-check in with often, to help her to calm down.

But the man jumped away from her.

And, if she could have placed him on his back in order to slide one arm under his knees, to raise him to *her* knee, and then to fold him against her breast—she would have.

He is the power and light representative for the district and he asked her for a list of all of the electrical items sold in the last six months.

So she finished recording the data, except that she confused several of the names of the customers, entering their first names as last names and this is one of her busiest days.

Another man came in to give her confidential information. And she said to him among other shrill things: *What do you mean? What do you mean? I can't. Come on. God.*

How does she fare at home?

Well, she prepared a variety cut for her supper, not a regular cut. It was a beef heart— the largest and least tender of these cuts. She sliced it very thin and then fried.

Later she squeezed the proper measure of hand cream into the palm of her hand and rubbed at her hands with her head bent low, because this is the way she does it, and with this new greasiness on her, she's wringing her hands in grief or in greediness or in both.

. . .

So . . . may the words of her mouth and the meditations of her heart be acceptable. *Come on, God!* Oh Lord. And her grabbiness.

CAPTURED!

———

"I am going to the doctor. I can't pay you!" the woman told the taxi driver. "You'll have to take me back home. I forgot my purse!"

"Now how do you think I got here?" she asked the nurse, whose reply was, "You floated."

Then there was her fleet exit before she took her turn.

The nurse quizzed other patients, "Did she have on a black coat?"

Someone said, "I thought it was red. She's still out there."

"Where was she?" said the nurse. "She must have been close to the building. I couldn't see her."

"Because of the umbrellas. Why doesn't she wait inside? Do you know her well?" a patient said.

"For fifteen years!"

"I can't go after her," said a man who was holding on to the cross piece of his crutch. There was nothing on his head for head protection.

On the avenue the woman's face is shot with rainwater. And she is named Eranthe Littleton, just so you know, and is diminutive.

Her shoulders are narrow, her arms are short and her hands undersize. Her natural hair color tends to brighten her. It is terra rosa or is that burnt sienna?

Her active mind speeds along because she is a sylph who loves the world and she rises in her life through her own merits.

And when the nurse finds her, I can easily foresee that Eranthe will offer to take her by the hand.

FINISHED BEING

———◆———

She looked with respect at a solid square of
cement-hued cement with a narrow frame
of black tar surrounding it and she asked herself why she had to do that.

WHAT IS GIVEN WITH PLEASURE AND RECEIVED WITH ADMIRATION?

———————

For her, sometimes the conjugation was a haphazard intertwining, with loose swings—other times more planned and positive.

All right. Good.

Why?—because now she is a grown woman and she has had a lot of intercourse with her husband, except that she has ended the marriage.

And things nearby her may prompt a recollection or tell a story.

On her stovetop, for example, an iron pot she owns has been scoured and scooped out even more than she has. And its sides meet its bottom in a wide curve to provide for efficient stirring and this pot offers her a hole of significance that is well-filled with bubbles of water and with light when the telephone rings.

"Ms. Polly Ann Willums?" the caller says, "I need to get in touch with Ms. Polly Ann Willums. Are you Ms. Polly Ann Willums?"

She answers no and also balks at the gruel in the offing that had been headed for the hot pot.

Outside she goes alongside the river to hear horns blowing and a bell ringing and she is drawn forward—but by what?

It could be the sun appearing, as if it were a lank strand of brass wire coiling.

It lights her way, and both the sky and the river are wavy and blue and she meets a friend by chance whose hair is newly auburn.

That's right. Her friend DeeDee Luck has topped herself off, so to speak, in a color resembling the onset of a fire and her friend is accompanied by her two small sons.

Since they are all on the ditch-side of the river, the bigger boy kneels down and throws up a handful of black mud.

"Oh, Tyler!" cries his mother, when Tyler sits down in the ooze. "You always get your way!"

The boy says, "*Ye-e-e-e!* I get my way," and

he is slapping at the soil and then Tyler extends the range of his antics.

He obtains an easy kind of rhythm that well expresses the isolation of individual people.

SHE'LL LOVE ME FOR IT

———◆———

There is often a part of the sky at nightfall
that she really enjoys, too, and the woman's
late father can be seen never suffering from
the waist up, hanging young and bland above
a sideboard in a portrait.

Just the same, this woman is bollixed by an
emotional problem and it's as if she smacks her
head against the wall until blood spurts out and
the color red is also vivid in the street where
she lives—where an equestrian statue has been
painted a pretty shade of it by vandals.

You see the woman's health began to give way because of that emotional problem.

It doesn't help that she eats heavily salted, dyed meat along with her eggs and irresponsible is not the right word for this.

The place in which she sleeps poorly is in the room across the passage from where she eats and we have the ability to get close to her gross movements, her ordinary life and to pick at her critically.

During lonely months the woman thought, *I touched him!* And we often observe this type of pining among primitive types.

And I saw her grieving, but I didn't think the world of her.

Where is her capacity for being a sly tease? For being playful?

Mind you, the portrait of her father features good flesh-painting and the technique was drawn from the methods of others—feathery touches.

What if the woman is dignified when she speaks?—and what if I am generous about her behind her back by suggesting that her structure— her long back muscles, her buttocks, shoulder blades, all of it—amounts to a great domestic landmark?—gracious and picturesque—that may stand up against a headwind while she overlooks the broad expanse of a river. She'll love me for it.

Will do.

SECRETLY TRY

———◆———

In bed at night she doubles back and then turns, as if she is on a course whose curves and bends she must follow.

And she has descended into the bed wearing a gown—and the cloth twists and climbs about her.

Her daughter also has her own idea of getting somewhere. She sits in the backyard swing, while crouched down, and she kicks.

She has been dubbed Little Mary, who

needs to regain strength, and she is currently her mother's burden.

But give this mother credit—she was speaking to a man while crossing the street the other day, and she was impressed with herself.

And when she spoke, she declared a purpose and such principles that we'd all be proud to honor.

And as the troop of people that the mother walked among went past several stone walls and hedges, and then past a house with a particularly complex face—the mother, of a sudden, gave up her pride in herself.

She looked dead into that face and felt that the house flaunted its royal arrogance when it refused to look directly back at her.

A laburnum in bloom and a fruit tree were equally aloof and my thought is that *all of these mothers* have to be decidedly hateful to someone, to somebody, to some persons.

So this mother of Little Mary approached a panel truck with its motor running and she was shocked by the truck's stretched-out posture.

But in time enough the truck shied away from her.

In this same district, the mother saw a house—brick below, shingles above—with all-over colors of red and gray and it displays a

variety of windows—one round—one's a verti-
cal, one horizontal.

And that house!

An important family lives in it and its over-
all effect is supple. It has a rounded roofline.

It is built so that its lower section is confident. Its upper zone is suspicious.

This living space shows off a nervous tem-
perament that could persist.

HOW HIGH?—THAT HIGH

H e had his stick that was used mostly to point at your head if your head wasn't held up proudly.

I still like that man—Holger! He had been an orphan!

He came up to me once because there was something about how I was moving my feet that wasn't according to the regulations or his expectations.

The room was a short wide room with a short wide window with plenty of artificial light.

On Holger's say-so, the girls stayed seated and we all crossed the room to ask them to dance and to make a bow.

I have never doubted the logic of it, but I was surprised I acted swiftly with my hair neatly water-combed, in my suit and my tie.

I liked her—the girl I asked—and she had bread breath from rye bread, my favorite—and my elbow needed to be up, my hand placed between her waist and her shoulder blades.

And when the music stopped, I took her back to her spot like a little man of the world, with no reason to complain. I returned to the other side of the room to wait until we'd move one place over to ask the next girl in the row to dance.

To this day—I keep up my ambition to meet guidelines.

Although tonight, to get to where my wife stood, I was probably stepping too quickly.

Had I made an irregular gesture, unforeseen? —because she pulled away quite thoroughly.

She said, *"You always latch on to me when I am about to yawn, and now I can't do it!"* And she lifted her chin, covered her mouth and tried again.

But after failing, she had that expression I know so well—that she is suffering, as she should, and for a better reason than I ever do.

Was she afraid of me? Why isn't she afraid of me?

To a great extent there is great value in her sour face, still capable of awing me.

Because she was dressed for a gala, her mouth was painted red. Her eyes were lined in black, her hair curled.

What all this reminds me of is a wise saying: "Do not use the contents of an unlabeled bottle—even if you think you remember what it contains."

One side of her face then seemed about to smile, as if she was also staring at me, smiling at me behind my back, yet nothing was funny.

I do not try to argue, reason or fight back with a person in this state, which is so similar a state to brave, balanced, grand.

TALE OF HUMAN ADVENTURE

———◆———

The woman cropped up and side by side we went afield, but will we ever find our golden plateau of sorts?

I don't forget how she once approached me—hunched—I was seated—and then she told me she loved me.

Please don't assume she's unappealing or that I'm not interested. She is a long-necked creature and there are subtle variations in the shadow patterns produced by her facial features.

She is easy to motivate and she shows genuine humility.

So with her along, I was bringing a porcelain jar—or it's a pot—to be corrected, mended.

There's a better word for *pot*. There are better words for any of my words.

Well, there are born storytellers and this story should certainly make every point clear, show an enthusiastic appreciation of all things beautiful, supply quickness of thought and even report climate changes.

Recently I had been unkind to Clara without reservation and as we proceeded, she crossed her arms over her waist, while a dog who was leashed at his ease, looked our way and held up its paw.

"I'm sorry," I said—and then the woman wore a smile and was turned toward me, one hand at her breast.

We skirted an exposed concrete building, an early skyscraper and finally arrived at the Queen Anne storefront where the proprietor greeted us—and other stylized humans of plaster and marble, as if alive, sat or stood on surfaces everywhere—a toddler. It was a winged boy.

One of these figures was actually a real girl with her back to us who was kneeling behind the counter. She must have been engaged in stock work or she was injured beyond reasonable wear. I told myself, *Don't look!*

Then I was making a good bargain and my item, as a matter of course, was examined.

My making things better brings an exhilaration that sticks in the memory.

"My responsibility does not extend to all losses," the proprietor said—"I want you to understand."

Another customer came in. "You are a very handsome couple," he told us. "But," he asked Clara, gesturing at me—*"Can you stand him?"*

Clara began to answer, but I cannot imagine not correcting her.

I pause here.

I think now and then of getting married, but have not done so.

Let me say, I wrote all of the above only to amuse myself.

Can you hear me?

The whole experience of writing this was enjoyable, as is the entire seriousness with which I take myself.

In the shop, a bust of Beethoven soon presented itself, and I felt a throb of confidence, while taking the measure of his enormous bulk.

I tried to tip it, to force him back a bit, but not to crack him.

Then up popped the specter, the kneeling girl from behind the counter.

I was completely shot to pieces thinking what I should do about *her*.

SIGHT SEE

———◆———

Point-blank up ahead was the Atlantic Ocean, but at this time it was lackluster from where we stood—still too big and navy, but not glossy.

"I won't swim," I said.

My friend said, "What did you say?" He was bound then to shout, *"Louder!"*

A mother leaned down to ask her little boy, "What does a cow say, Zachariah? *Moo?*"

"I don't feel well," I said.

But I was quieted by my friend.

What was that bird? There was something melodic coming out of it.

I wished we could have been swept right along, because heaped-up human activities close by were packed too thickly in a small greasy place.

Were we simply roaming forward toward a northern region, distant from our own?

I actually liked the ride to the other end of town, although on the bus I was nauseated.

We had lunch in a café with small-paned windows. The decoration inside I thought was intended to inspire fervor for food plus awe.

Where did I end up? Not yet anywhere near intellect.

IT'S SO EFFORTFUL

———————◆———————

Claus's whole hand, face-down, slid under my bottom during the taxicab ride.

"Shall I come over tonight?" he asked me.

That man has such an extraordinary ability to get close to ordinary life. I've tried.

He was in a chair at my kitchen table and I climbed in behind him onto the chair, my arms around his front, not for long.

He told me, in the bedroom, to lie down on the floor on my back and he got on top and hooked his feet around my ankles. That didn't last.

So when I wait for the right moment and then I hop on top of Claus, my legs are spread and bent like a frog's.

If only I could climb Claus like a tree. I've seen movies of young boys climbing palm trees. They embrace the trunk, and then they march right up, or is it that they shimmy? That's just about it. They lean in instead of dangling.

Can you imagine all of the juice the palm tree has to transport all the way to its palm fronds way up there?—so that the tree is pulling liquid from the earth in a major way and the shaft itself is so spindly.

And yet my entire nature and all my instincts fail to clasp Claus for even one quiver—before I have to come right back down from there.

FLOWERS, BIRDS,
AND GARDENS

———◆———

Jane says, "It should be impossible, because I did kind of like how it was I had it before ... the wooden floor going through on its own, and the furniture just floating. But I like the rug so much."

And if Jane's sofa had a tongue—the carpet would be the tongue that the sofa sticks out.

It ejects itself out from under while it offers up its garden pattern on a red background.

At lunch, Jane tells Jay that she is still in agreement with everything she's decided recently and that this is the first time she has ever felt this way.

As for Jay, he has digested Jane's beef patties and he never knows if he can, and then if he does, he is so grateful to his body.

Jane goes into the kitchen to chop food for the next meal, and when she comes back out, Jay says, "Oh, I didn't kill him . . ." about the big fly they had surprised, while it was flexing its legs on top of the pie's meringue.

"He isn't swarming around here, is he?" says Jane, and she extends her lower lip. "He's on your arm." Then the fly flees.

"Oh," she says, "I have to wind the clock. Did it stop? Yes, it did. And even if you wind it, it doesn't start willingly. You have to talk to it. I usually have a broken-off toothpick and I give the swing wheel a little nudge. It worked!"

So Jay thinks that Jane might be ready to joke—that she is a nice person—and then she demands that Jay go to the market *toute suite* to get them a big tub of margarine spread.

And so, she's sort of soured things between them, Jay thinks—forever, or for now.

By the way, Jane has spent time in France where she had an admirer, but for some reason she decided Jay was a better choice and she is blithe now and revived when Jay starts out the door.

One might watch Jay on the threshold as he coughs and merges into the aggregate—into the unthought-through miscellany.

A moth is stuck or resting flat-out on his window screen—a weak flyer that requires the wind to bear it aloft and forward.

On the lawn, in the park meanwhile, a tiny child chases an idling flock of pigeons. He keeps running into them so that they flap and plunge, sometimes they soar.

Aha, they're not sure of themselves . . .

Usually birds appear to know what they are doing.

MAKING SPLENDID

———◆———

The woman's eyes are small and brown, but naturally we've all seen a lot of eyes like those eyes.

And, there are two windows above her head for us to look up and out from, but no rococo clouds can be seen inside of these jambs and sills and we would expect the sky, at this time of day, to be a foreordained gray color, a predictable blue or white, and it is.

The woman's heart was not pumping helpfully and she was saying, "Everything else

I am throwing away . . . we don't need . . . I'll have to look at the table. Harold!—I've already had the cake! No, thank you, and we need a yellow marker."

Her mouth is mushroom-pink and the quaint tongue-and-groove boarding of their walls is a mustard yellow—which color the couple experiences as old and warm and they are both old and a bit whipped.

Albeit, when the woman begins a sentence, she often says the words *Harold and I* with zest.

And she is capable of vehement flushing— so that when she is hysterical, or let's say—she just overreacts, her face is fuchsia.

This woman's fine feverish hue makes me think of happy times and it's high time, for me, for that—and she's such a good sport.

OUTCOME

——◆——

The wife is pretty sure she should admire her husband except that he is usually away on a horse, and, of course, he has to take care of his horses. So she keeps in mind the stylish, hatted, back view of him.

He likes to think of his wife in brief bursts. She is a distant splash, a distant booming.

He has—I don't know how to put it. He has a certain way about him that is elegant, but as far as having money—he really doesn't have any.

He works as a cowboy and he doesn't want to stop while he rides from one location to the next. He claims that he can ride his horse and sleep at the same time.

And what sort of work does his wife do?

She is a clerk—but why does she so easily give in when people prove her wrong? She pays bills, does filing and cannot recognize she is capable of making beautiful mistakes.

Her husband, on the other hand, out on the range, goes to sleep confident that he has done the best job he can do.

Often though, in his wife's presence, he is just too brightly lit—or it's something—

She feels the need to turn aside to ward off his chin and the beard, his mouth, his nose and the slanted eyebrows.

And yet she might say, "Did you hear what I said?"

And, he'll say, "I heard—" and he will repeat some trivia.

Perhaps one of them is a liar, and the other is too readily humiliated.

At night the wife pulls back the block-printed Indian bedcover.

If only it was her bed of roses.

So, on the floor lies their standard—their banner—a soft, cotton rag rug.

It is the faintest impression of what might never have been enough—a thing of the past, so very thin-edged and arranged freshly.

HARRIET MOUNCE

I was able to get Harriet Mounce to shriek and I think I must have thought any shriek would do.

When she first stood there naked, I remember she was solemn or she looked annoyed or was she really pained? But she did seem to like me. The cues—she had really focused her eyes on me and she had smiled while on her haunches by the hearth a bit earlier.

Because she is a brunette, the sight of the

crop of red hair above her pubis surprised me very much.

So how do I put this?

Her raptures aside, she lost interest in me quickly, although she sent me notes and letters. She said she knew that the tragedy of losing her would be a shock for me—that I am always in her mind in a nice way—that is, my personal sorrow is present for her. I should please accept her deepest sympathy—that she cannot help sending me her understanding sympathy.

There was just so much pleasure in store when I was a boy and I was resourceful.

Once a year my brother and I sneaked into a fair where they handed out free samples of our favorite sweets and we were gifted with these strips of aluminum from a toothpaste company!

If you ran your thumbnail across the strip— you could hear a voice singing *Use Vademecum!*

The woman sang the words quickly or I could get her to croak this out slowly, over and over.

POPPING

———◆———

She selects a deep-dark violet eggplant that is not shriveled—green beans that are not dirty or coarse—a cucumber that's not too thick or puffy.

This plaid-dressed lady's voice is faint and sing-song and why does she tell herself things that she already knows?—as if she is talking to a stranger—*Any avocados that aren't soft? Fresh celery? Do you have fresh grapes?*

A man the lady sees lifts a moon glow pear, and although its skin can be bitter, he presses it to his lips. And this marvelous pear, after he puts it back down, is competent to shed its aura all over a kiwi.

As a matter of fact, each and every color here at Shim's is popping around. And not merely a few of us can be distracted by all of this—the history of art teaches us.

As she dawdles near a shop that sells odd-ball crockery and other possible gifts—the lady receives a wink from Max Hinks. And since she had long wished for this eye contact—she is now well-gratified.

Oh, the eggplant?—she'll dice it and fry it, and until then it will be refrigerated and covered to prevent drying—same for the beans. The cucumber will be slashed nearly instantly.

And during this era, all injury to this lady beyond reasonable wear—all losses shall be made good to her satisfaction and when she is injured or lost—the responsibility for her shall be widespread.

This was only the case last year, when her life was not so fast-paced and gripping as it is now. Now there are persons at her side timing her vitals—until, sorry—until she is dead.

She did tend to her husband when he was ill, and she was nice to him, although they had arguments about money.

Money is foremost in her husband's mind and what he likes best are durable and practical things—stainless steel tableware and the like, that bear no resemblance to his late wife.

He is especially fond of his Waring two-slot, light duty toaster that was produced with no hazardous material.

It is electric, 120 volts, 950 watts and is considered by many to be the greatest toaster ever made.

STICK

———◆———

How best to touch these woody objects or a person?

She batted together the parts of the sycamore stick she had broken in two and then made of them the self-important capital letter T—and she spun one.

She rolled the stick over her thumb and then she tried for greater twirling speed, as she sat on the park bench that bore a personalized inscribed plaque dedicated to MY DEAREST NANCY.

She is not that Nancy, nor is she a beloved

Lara yet, who might have a plan that aims to shore up her heart and her strength, with tools and accessories that support her life in the early-evening-burning-summertime in the city.

Just do it, she thought, and she put the stick through its paces again. Its athleticism, its success, it seemed to her, could foretell her own. So that it pained her when she had to throw the sticks away.

She stood suddenly to walk on, but instead paused to watch girls at their hopscotch game— *hop*, *hop*, *hop*, *jump*, and *bow*. They bowed down when they stooped to retrieve their pebble marker.

To revive her sense of purpose, the woman was out on the avenue, hugging her little body.

Her feet felt pinched inside her shoes, her best shoes. Her stylized hair fell down her shoulders. What else?

She put one foot precisely in front of the other, just like the old adage prescribed—just to test what that would feel like.

Would this help her to suppose that she was any more determined—any more capable of taking care of herself?

She prayed nobody was paying her any mind, as this gambit caused her hips to sidle this way that way, lewdly.

In her own home she had no witness.

At bedtime, these days, she entered the room alone in which she and the dour Don Super had once slept together. He had so often recoiled from her.

Well, oughtn't she be able to reach out to a trusted person with the same confidence she has when she takes up a bar of soap or nudges a chair back?

From a distance, she used to watch Super's penis rise, because he had made it clear that he had no need for her participation. And although his appendage essentially floated in place—it also looked ready and able to propel itself.

What this woman decided on Fifth Avenue, in the here and now, is that she ought to plow forward and *skip*!

She should not permit her arms and hands to drag down like wet noodles.

ONE MUGGY SPRING

———◆———

She was free from upset briefly when she heard the syncopations and the suspensions of time—the soft background music at the eatery that promised to relieve vexation. It was well blended and the rich harmony involved a bassoon.

She was there with good old Jim, in the springtime, who asked her, "Do you still have intercourse? Do you bleed?"

But in real life Jim did not say anything like

that and his penis was not yet sliding around her or poking.

So their moment did not become explosive and they ate their dumplings.

One of them was eager to take the paper wrapping off of the drink straw because it is the easiest thing to have trouble with, but not to fail at.

The woman sums up her son and daughter thusly when Jim inquires—Teddy is slothful and Paige is satisfied to be average in every category and now she can't seem to do anything right—she is dying.

And yet the sound of the woman's indignation—its clip and its tenor—if Jim could only disregard the words—was not unappealing to his ear.

Still, Jim was fearful of what the woman might tell him next or that she might ask him a shaming question.

He was a little bit atremble further into the meal, when he sweetened up his coffee.

The woman watched him pour sugar in and stir. He poured more sugar in and stirred and next he poured in more sugar and he stirred.

As she drove herself home, the woman was hardly aware of anything except for the suggestion of roadway, on account of the misty drizzle.

In these warm months—the grass and the

trees and even the people—their houses and their cars and bicycles—vanished in the fog, and it was promising. And the trees were safely tucked in. Their roots were rallying in the soil, in this coil.

Would the woman also take a turn for the better in her last decade?

She felt a breeze at the top of her head while driving—and since the car windows were tightly shut, she marveled at the source of the tiny gust.

But now she had a dull ache there, in her scalp. Was that sensation *arousal*?

Well, then the rain became heavier, and it made of her car's body a drum skin that produced a low-pitched, dry sound, much like applause—that is not apropos here, *not* fitting.

Because plainly there are the woman's shortcomings to consider, when one compares her to other mothers—or to the huge central pool of mothers, or to the huge central pool of persons who have demonstrated that quality—*pathos*.

The woman leans forward. She can't see—can't see well enough to drive safely.

She sees only roughly splashed grays.

She did not brake the car in the middle of the road. Rather, she continued driving, while weighing the meaning of her bony hands barely holding the wheel.

MASTER OF THE BLAST

————◆————

That's how bright the sky was! A woman's lilac dress somehow picked up greenish hues as she was chewing and chewing one biteful.

And was she even hungry as she squeezed her hands together under her chin, so that her knuckles pulsed?—as she kept on with her snapping and gouging and delving into what was both pliable and crisp.

It was not easily done—and then a boy who was with her sneezed.

"God bless you!" I said.

"Why?" the boy asked. Another one of his sneezes followed that expanded and rolled, but drew no salute.

The chewer had stopped her chewing and thanked the server for offering her more coffee—coffee that I could see had strength, unexpected darkness.

And with a deep, indwelling smile, the server said, "Perfect."

Then I coughed abruptly and the cough was a buglelike three-parter.

There followed some barely audible drumming on a tabletop from a man who was enthusiastically engaged with his percussion.

The woman told her boy, "Well then, I want you—" as the boy cowered and as the sound of my own tearing, with my teeth, into my toast, interfered with my hearing any more of his mother's scolding.

It is such a challenge to express exuberances in disrupted areas.

I folded my restaurant tab in half, tore it at the center of the fold. I held it like a cigarette, then I rolled the two ends over my fingers and put my mouth to it and I blew. This didn't work. I was out of practice, but it needs to be flimsy paper, because then when the air strikes across the torn slot, the paper starts to vibrate in the airstream and it makes a big noise.

There! Then I did it! It's not always one hundred percent.